KT-155-801

MARGARET MAHY

THE HORRENDOUS HULLABALOO

Illustrated by Patricia MacCarthy

Shetland Library

Margaret Mahy

The Horrendous hullabaloo

173593

PUFFIN BOOKS

SHETLAND LIBRARY

There was once a cheerful old woman who kept house for her nephew, Peregrine – a pirate by profession.

Every morning she put on her pirate pinafore, poured out Peregrine's ration of rum, picked up his socks, and petted his parrot. She worked day in, day out, keeping everything shipshape.

Meanwhile, her pirate nephew went out to parties every night, though he never once asked his aunt or his parrot if they would like to go with him.

Whenever his aunt suggested that she and the parrot might want to come too, Peregrine replied, "You wouldn't enjoy pirate parties, dear aunt. The hullabaloo is horrendous!"

"But I like horrendous hullabaloos!" exclaimed the aunt. "And so does the parrot."

"When I come home from sea I want a break from the parrot," said Peregrine, looking proud and piratical. "And if I took my aunt to a party, all the other pirates would laugh at me."

"Very well," thought his aunt, "I shall have a party of my own."

Without further ado she sent out masses of invitations written in gold ink. Then she baked batch after batch of delicious rumblebumpkins while the parrot hung upside down on a pot plant, clacking its beak greedily.

No sooner had Peregrine set off that evening on another night's hullabaloo than his aunt, shutting the door behind him, peeled off her pirate pinafore and put on her patchwork party dress.

"Half past seven!" she called to the parrot. "We'll soon be having a horrendous hullabaloo of our own!"

Then she opened the windows and sat waiting for the guests to come, enjoying the salty scent of the sea, and the sound of the waves washing around Peregrine's pirate ship, out in the moonlit bay.

"Half past eight!" chimed the clock. The pirate's aunt waited.

"Half past nine!" chimed the clock. The pirate's aunt still waited, shuffling her feet and tapping her fingers.

"Half past ten!" chimed the clock. The rumblebumpkins were in danger of burning. No one, it seemed, was brave enough to come to a party at a pirate's house. The pirate's aunt shed bitter tears over the rumblebumpkins.

Suddenly the parrot spoke. "I have lots of friends who love rumblebumpkins," she cackled. "Friends who aren't put in a panic or petrified by pirates – friends who would happily help with a hullabaloo!"

"Well, what are you waiting for?" cried the pirate's aunt. "Go and fetch them at once!"

Out of the window the parrot flew, while the aunt mopped up her tears and patted powder on her nose.

Almost at once the night air was filled with flapping and fluttering. The sea swished and sighed. The night breeze smelled of passion fruit, pineapples and palm trees. In through the open windows tumbled the patchwork party guests, all screeching with laughter. They were speckled, they were freckled; they were streaked and striped like rollicking rags of rainbow. All the parrots in town had come to the aunt's party.

"Come one, come all!" the aunt cried happily.

The parrots cackled loudly, breaking into a bit of a sing-song. So loud was the sing-song that the pirate's neighbours rushed out of their houses, prepared for the worst.

"What a horrendous hullabaloo!" they cried in amazement.

The aunt invited them all to feast richly on her rumblebumpkins, and to join her in a wild jig. She was having a wonderful time.

When Peregrine arrived home later that night, his house was still ringing with leftover echoes of a horrendous hullabaloo. The air smelled strongly of rumblebumpkins, and the floor was covered in parrot feathers.

"Aunt!" he called crossly. "Come and tidy up at once."

But there was no one at home for, at that very moment, his aunt, still wearing her patchwork party dress, was stealing away on Peregrine's own pirate ship.

Over the moonlit sea she was sailing, with parrots perched all over her, making a horrendous hullabaloo. As they sailed off in search of passion fruit, pineapples and palm trees, it was impossible to tell where the aunt left off and the parrots began.

So, left on his own, with a grunt and a groan Peregrine put on the pirate pinafore and tidied up for himself.

THE HORRENDOUS HULLABALOO